Willie
Masters'
Lonesome
Wife

DALKEY ARCHIVE PRESS
CHAMPAIGN / LONDON / DUBLIN

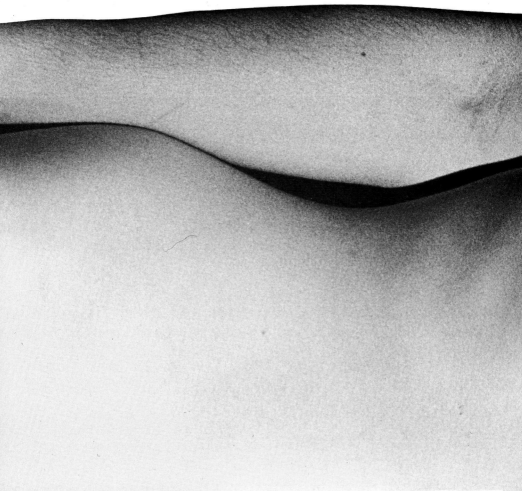

First published as *TriQuarterly* Supplement Number Two, 1968
First Dalkey Archive edition, 1989
second printing, 1992
third printing, 1998
fourth printing, 2014

ISBN: 1-56478-212-3   LC 89-11724

Partially funded by grants from
the Illinois Arts Council, a state agency.

www.dalkeyarchive.com

Printed on permanent/durable acid-free paper

Willie Masters' Lonesome Wife

BY WILLIAM H. GASS

he'd love him even if his head weren't shiny. I'll be a little mouse of a woman, blond and skinny, and there'll be rings on my belly where men have set down drinks. It would be nice to be a poker table—all those male knees under you—and wear green baize like a grass dress and turn my body up to the cool backs of playing cards, the cool rain of chips. Phil he said his name was . . . Was he? They were always Phil. *His hair was the only illumination in the room. Its smooth slope lit her breasts.*

It is certainly amazing what brilliantine can do.

Or they were Jim or George or Frank or Harry. Gentlemen gave themselves all sorts of pseudonyms, as though she cared or would ever tattle. They ought to name their noses like they named their pricks. Why not their ears too?—they frequently stuck out. This is my morose Slav nose, Czar Nicholas. And these twins in my mirror, Reuben and Anthony, they have large soft lobes.

She had so wanted lobes when she was young. To dangle diamonds from, and pearls in petals of silver, spills of crimson glass or wheels of polished jade or even jasper, a match for her

hair. Waiting for her lobes to grow was like having an unde-
scended testicle or a flat chest, she supposed—when, for god's
sake, you wondered, would something show up—and she peered
into the circle of the shaving glass which slanted on her bureau,
tugging at her ears until they ached.

Her own nose was buttony.

Suppose, for instance, a stranger were to—oh, say you're laughing uproariously, and that's the occasion for it—spit in your mouth, god forbid. Still, daily, they do worse. So here you are, you've cracked your face across—ha ha ha-ing—and someone—some enemy, some social scientist, some polisher of singular skills—fires it in suddenly. Well you've always had your own wash working for you, sloshing about—an inland sea foaming up against its rocks (how grand that's put, how grand), and you don't mind it. You don't go hithering and thithering, do you? moaning, do you? god, my god, my head is leaking, lord, my head is leaking through my mouth, my god, and down my throat and past my shoulders, all those tubes, good lord, and toward my shoes? In that case, then, you must be friendly to it. You're old chums. But hawk blind on a table and you'll never tell your spatter from a thousand. Queens. Boyfriends. Bums. If you have an experimental twist, try this: expectorate into a glass—sufficiently—twelve times should do it. Do not tarry. Drink the spittle. Analyze your reluctance. And wonder why they call saliva the sweet wine of love.

There was never any doubt about my bosom, buddy; breasts as big as your butt there, nipples red and rubbery. A regular dairy, my daddy always said. **Babs' Sweet Buttery.** The smart ass. The hairy smart ass. Well, a smirk to his memory. This plump little lady, he used to say, shot up like a weed when she was eight. What a smart ass. May the tines in his skull ache. A milk-weed, he'd shout, and then he'd tickle my tummy and shatter with laughter. You're going to amount to something, baby, he'd say, shaping his hands, the smart ass; you're going to be as big this sway as you are the other. This

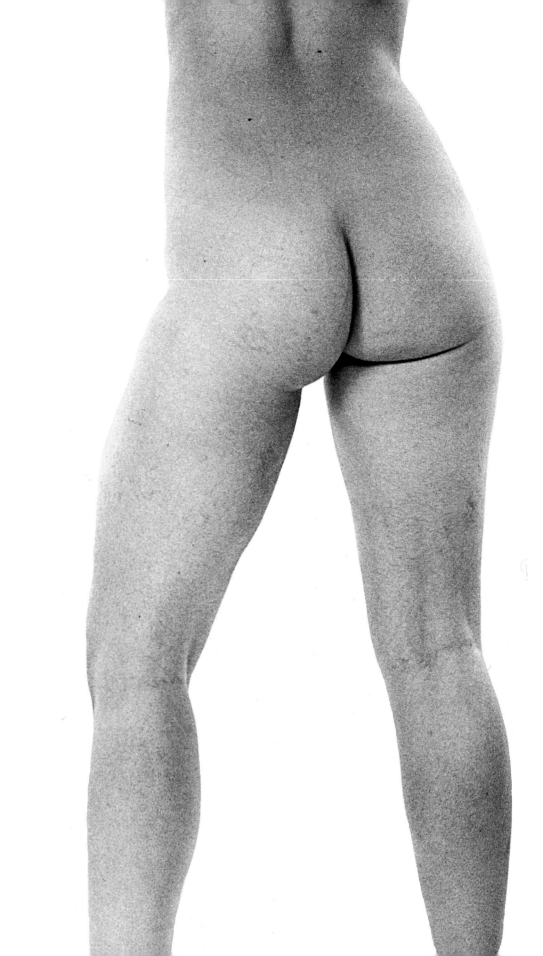

sway, see? he'd say, and fold in delight. Now he's giving his
worms gas, the beery s.o.b.

I can't complain. You're supposed to be lonely—getting
fucked, I guess that's what will happen. Time out from picture
magazines, the pattern books, no breather for a cigarette or
laying out of solitaires or swallowing beer or vacuuming the
rug, I dream, invent, and I imagine. The wallpaper's filled with
blowing trees, the shades are rolled, my tumbler's caked, the
radio has come unplugged, a heavy mist has roped the hills,
and the marigolds rot in their vase. I dream like Madame
Bovary. Only I don't die during endings, I never die. They fall
asleep on me and shrivel up. I write the finis for them, close the
covers, shelf the book. But I don't understand what excites them
in the first place. It's nothing about me; it's not me they love.
They could have had their cocks shout through a toilet tube for
all the difference they would notice in the crowing. Except, I
think, imagining, for them, is like a babyhood disease, embarrassing to have past ten; and so they need some flesh-like
copy, some sexy pix and rubber lover, a substitute in plasti-
goop or blanket-cloth to keep them safe, to keep them clean
of fact and fancy. Well, I'm busty, passive, hairy, and will
serve. Departure is my name. I travel, dream. I feel sometimes
as if I were imagination (that spider goddess and thread-
spinning muse)—imagination imagining itself imagine. Then I
am as it is, reflecting on my own revolving, as though a record
might take down its turning and in that self-responsive way
comprise a song which sings its singing back upon its notes as
purely as a mirror, and like a mirror endlessly unimages itself,
yet is none the less an image (just as much a woman, gauzy muse
and hot-pants goddess quite the same), for all that generosity—
for all that giving of itself and flowing constantly away.

sway, see? he'd say, and fold in delight. Now he's giving his worms gas, the beery s.o.b.

I can't complain. You're supposed to be lonely—getting fucked. I *guess* that's what will happen. Time out from picture magazines, the pattern books, no breather for a cigarette or laying out of solitaires or swallowing beer or vacuuming the rug. I dream, invent, and I imagine. The wallpaper's filled with blowing trees, the shades are rolled, my tumbler's caked, the radio has come unplugged, a heavy mist has roped the hills, and the marigolds rot in their vase. I dream like Madame Bovary. Only I don't die during endings. I never die. They fall asleep on me and shrivel up. I write the *finis* for them, close the covers, shelf the book. But I don't understand what excites them in the first place. It's nothing about me; it's not *me* they love. They could have had their cocks shout through a toilet tube for all the difference they would notice in the crowing. Except, I think, imagining, for them, is like a babyhood disease, embarrassing to have past ten; and so they need some flesh-like copy, some sexy pix and rubber lover, a substitute in plasti-goop or blanket-cloth to keep them safe, to keep them clean of fact and fancy. Well, I'm busty, passive, hairy, and will serve. Departure is my name. I travel, dream. I feel sometimes as if I *were* imagination (that spider goddess and thread-spinning muse)—imagination imagining itself imagine. Then I *am* as it *is,* reflecting on my own revolving, as though a record might take down its turning and in that self-responsive way comprise a song which sings its singing back upon its notes as purely as a mirror, and like a mirror endlessly unimages itself, yet is none the less an image (just as much a woman, gauzy muse and hot-pants goddess quite the same), for all that generosity—for all that giving of itself and flowing constantly away.

It's called the wine of love because, when drunk, it signifies acceptance. That's my theory. There's no woman who's not, deep inside her, theoretical. That's why we love, in men, not them, but place and reputation —money, honor, age, effects, and aura—radiation; not them, but their love, we love—our idea and transubstantiating notion of them. That's my theory. Most people are distressed, honestly enough, by their own dirt. Imagine the shit of a lifetime packed in tubs. It would be small comfort knowing it was yours. Still, the dirt of others is even more distressing. Pick another's nose, for instance. Proof enough? Well, that's my theory. We get used to it—our own—we get used to it. Soldiers get used to it. They get used to death, distress, and the dirt of others. Mothers, of course, get used to it. We whores get used to it. But all of us are harlots to ourselves, and soldiers: we get used to it—our dead breath and dying eyelight, bare basins and odd bodies—used to living in a trench.

It surprised her, under the circumstances, to remember how that fellow's nose had felt, the railroad conductor's, when he tried to kiss her between the cars—they were going to Gary— jabbing her cheek like an icicle, both of them swaying and jouncing—he must have been short, she was only a kid—at the same time shouting in her ear for her address while his stiff cap nearly scalped her—his nose was cold as a dog's nose, sharp as a stick—and she'd thought: love? no thanks, none of that gicky bumpydump for me, I'd rather turn into a roach right now, this instant, absolutely, and live on crumbs from candy wrappers kicked beneath the seats, I wouldn't care, and be completely curtained in by sweaty calves and dirty trousers, even if it was forever, absolutely, I wouldn't care; *still she must have had her destination pinned to her coat, the confident way he'd grabbed her, and she'd thought, flattered for a moment:* lust for me? nah ... golly! *until his cap had struck her like a cleaver; and it really had been a rehearsal, most of it, the jouncing and the ramming, the torrent of noise* (it's like living by a rapids or a fall, the way they huff and heave, you can't hear yourself think), *sure, it must have been a rehearsal, for what had her life been since but bumpydump . . . bumpydump and gicky.*

Feet now—feet are notably ugly—and don't they stand for the whole of us? Bent and knobby calloused things, hid in our shoes like solitary prisoners out of the light, dungeoned in their own stink and tread upon like a soft pavement of slaves—ai! a soft pavement of slaves! **let me away to Asia!—or, as in ancient days, driven through the dust like a pair of oxen or great drays over cobbles, they were naturally the first choice of our holy religion, weren't they? for washing, weren't they? for humbling . . . and for saintly love.**

Until my flesh began to lose its grip, I danced in the blue light with the best, and then I married Willie so I could dance the same dance still, the dance I'm dancing now, and not feel lonely, for Willie's eyes have all the human glow the spot had, or Phil's hair, here, has. Why, I've been hugged more warmly by the couches in hotels, and a zipper's bitten me with greater passion. Who makes me better love in bed? the bed does. Oh, we danced—divesting ourselves—and the comedians cracked jokes between their teeth like nuts. So every Peter has a peter, Charlie? Yeah, to make wee-wee, Joe. As it grows thick, they call it dick. Yeah, to make wow-wee, Charlie—**WOW-WEE**!

She giggled. Her lover lurched eagerly, scraping her skin. Why don't they shave when they should? John Thomas sounded awfully grown, like a lumberjack's. It would be agreeable, certainly, if they arranged them as to size and age, breeding, blood, or social position; then skill, too, would be sensible—Percy for some sorts, Raphael for others—*though she found it hard to believe they ever thought of anything, just got stiff like you'd catch your death in a raw wind, or weary, out too late, resistance thin, came down with flu, and had to force the phlegm from their noses before they could breathe again. She'd never met a Leonard or a Leonardo: ah, the aqueduct and the flying machine, the catapult. He drew them beautifully, in and out. No, a minor illness was what it was. Well, it wasn't catching, though it made her sick clear through with disappointment. Boris, maybe, or Prince Myshkin. In the old days, when she was young, she'd released their manhoods in the sun where she could see, like opening a cage. How uncomfortable they looked, how strange. She had no skill in the beginning; there was that jerky zip and eager fumble first . . . unpackaging a stubborn birthday. Ah, there you are, Feodor—Feodor Chaliapin.*

I used to write the scripts myself. I stole from the best, from the classiest greats, from books that only came in sets. They laughed just the same—for me or Gogol—they would yaw-yaw just the same. There's a fellow—a fellow—there's a fellow who says—to a real skinny girl—there's a fellow who says: you're an udder disappointment. And then the skinny girl says: I pricktickily don't like you either. Prick–tick — i l y , she says, giving his fly a long hard stare. That was a wow—that show. Well I'd be blond and skinny if I could. It would be a change: to vibrate like a wire, not bobble like a pudding. It doesn't help to think of yourself as a kind of pocket hankie either. Screw—they say, **screw**—what an idea! did any of them ever? It's the lady who wooves and woggles. Nail—bang!—sure—**nail** is nearer theirs.

She felt the terror of terminology.

Why aren't there any decent words?

There's this tall thin sad-faced guy with the loose trousers and the wide suspenders who's been camping under a crumply hat. And a drum going bum bum bum, bim-a-mum-bum. A big busting girl in a tight dress waltzes by. It's me. Me. Slow

slow and easy. Revolving her haunches. Clack! the stick strikes the rim of the drum, and his pants—the tall thin sad-faced fellow's pants—bulge; they shoot straight out. He's now as wide one way as he's long the other. Then the flat blond struts past. In a quick stiff trot. Bimly bimly bim. The piano runs at high, and his bulge—the sad fellow's bulge—goes bang like a balloon —no—it goes hush or shush like a balloon—a farting balloon— beg your pardon—zuzzzz—and he says to her: you're an udder disappointment.

Is that snow, love, clinging to the limbs of the trees, or warm sleeves of light instead?

I suppose they call their twiggy little wonder by different names in different parts of the world. No, I've got it wrong— remembering. Her bosom is all air, the busty one's bosom is, all air, and they pop when he grabs her; first one pops and then the other— **pop** —and then *his* does— **pop** —and he says: you're an udder disappointment.

Yeah.

Saintly love. Kiss my foot. Kiss the rubbered ends of canes, eh? Might as well, it doesn't matter. Not to them. All men alike, all equal, cash or god, it doesn't matter, that's not love—whore's love neither saintly love —but when you bring that foot to lip because it is that foot, that lip, because you want more than accept, why then . . . and I could touch those rubbered tips, if I had loved, if ever I had loved, in such a way that soles could not be more alive upon that blindman . . . ah yes, those, when I should touch them, he should feel the rush of my caress across the whole length of his cripple's sticks as though they were his only avenues and scopes of feeling; were, yes, were his eyes out there, for feet and motivation . . . so, when I should touch them, give my kiss, it would be as if I'd made him see my love entire in a vision, yes, me, laughing lonesomely and screwing oomfy whoozis on the sofa.

So every bitty bugger has a fugger. I dub you Roger. Juan. Or Otto. Breasts like a boy, the flat one never wore a star, and they were wild for her, she was a wow. We called her Merrie Cherrie; her green dress hung as straight as a drape; desire, in shivering waves, rose like heat. Cherrie says she's a bird lover. Well now, are you, I say, are you a bird lover? Oh, she says, oh I certainly am; birds, I love birds. Well now, I say, that's swell, Cherrie, that's sure swell, and what is your favorite bird, dearie; what bird do you love best? Oooh, Cherrie says, oooh, the red-headed woodpecker. Then there's laughter among the animals, jocularity in the jaw's hinge—the porcelain hilarity of teeth. We're always supposed to admire it, like a pet, though we're just a plate put down for their Rin-Tin-Tins to muzzle in. *She felt the horn sounding as she plumply turned.* Boom. Ba. TaTeeTa. Boom. Wovveling in and in. Eric? Morris? How is Babs today, and how are Babs' boobs? Nikolai. Habib. Albert. Paul. Bathed in blue. *She had heard somewhere that semen softens the skin.* Clarence. Horace. A violinist must care for his hands. What would you call a rhino, finely trained? I wouldn't call it Calvin. Calvin's a cad's name. And Gus is lower class. A pianist must take care for his hands. Charles. Christopher. Rise, Sir Habib, Knight of the Scrotum. That was in another skit. Pat and Mike—both balls—two wrinkled old retainers. Rise, Sir Something or Other, something dirty, the fat one says, I dub you Knight of the Round—what? round . . .? round . . .? round . . .? *She was eloquent, the way she walked, hands on her hips.* And it rises, sure, it rises, shoots straight out. Pat and Mike: to designate a politician's jowls. Gunnar. For the family hippo. *She taps him on the shoulder with a sausage. He's kneeling in front of her, facing her navel. Rise, Sir Dick, she says, or something, tapping right and left.* I dub you Peter, sir, Knight of the Round . . . why can't I think? A surgeon must care for his hands. A drummer must care for his bams. Why can't I remember? All she was was string and tassels, tossing string and tassels, a storm so strange you would have thought the snow drove the wind—trees flew wildly from their leaves—and I wouldn't have minded having an Ed or an Albert up her snug myself. Myself. Gotthold's elaborate. Abraham. It's six o'clock in Habibsburg. James, Jan, Joseph, Harold, John. Say, take it easy, kiddo, that's me. But can you imagine any woman thinking: I've Phyllis folded up my in-between? It's not such a bad idea, though. I might call mine . . . let's see . . . Corinne. If you had nice pleasant names for yourself all over, you might feel more at home, more among friends . . . if you ever were at home with people, that is . . . with friends. Clara. For an eye. It's some sort of savage's error—reading humanity in—so if you liked flowers better, you could try them. Buttercup? Four O'Clock? Bleeding Heart? Daisy? Oh doesn't he think I'm having a good time though. James, Jan, Joseph, Gerald, John: you're the toilets I pee down. I've spent my life in my arms, yet how well do I know them? Do you know yours, Fred, now my lap's around them? Clara has a cinder in her. I'm an utter stranger to my elbows, no wonder they're chapped. Is that your name? Fred? Well, hell, they're just trousers. I've seen a thousand empty trousers. Christ, they're all empty, when it comes to that. I must think of some names for my toes.

Timothy, Terence, Titus, Tom: one has the penis I'll try on; one has the staff that will strike from the South; another the laugh that I'll put in my mouth; one has a sickness to finish me: Tom, Titus, or Terence, or Timothy.

Somebodyvitch the barber and his missus in her wrapper, miming three langorous yawns, begin their roll and coffee breakfast. It is obvious from the flesh which shows between the flaps of her loosely hanging gown that she is naked. The audience is served soft mounds of bust and generous helpings of her fatty thighs before she settles to her paper. Played by me. She is a bitch. Well the woman is always the heavy. The husband, the barber, Ivan, is a wizened runt whose purplish cheeks have sunk against his teeth and whose eyes wink. Worry has sloped his shoulders and rounded his skull like a stone in a stream. There is a sign on the stage, tacked to a striped phallic pole, informing the audience in terms too corny to recall that Ivan is a barber and lets blood for a fee. Sammy— billed outside as the Vulgar Bulgar—slits his bun with an enormous cardboard razor we've provided. He carefully parts the lips of the cut with his fingers. Can it be he's burned himself? His fingers fly apart, the roll falls. Ivan grimaces, then shrugs. Nevertheless he regains his breakfast calmly and peeks la-de-da in the bun. Ah but not another moment passes before he's drawn up fiercely to it and is peering purposefully in. Dear me. Now he's really angry. There's a foreign something in his bread, no doubt about it, an alien substance—what? Finally, the crack nearly pinching his nose, he stares in astonishment and stupefaction. His head withdrawn, he winks; he knuckles his eyes. He smiles stupidly at the audience. He shrugs. He looks inside again. He is dumfounded, flabbergasted. Though his eyes pop, he cannot believe what he sees. He shuts the bun with force, with finality. He wags his head. He stands. He groans his length. He sits. He picks up the roll. He crosses his legs. He uncrosses his legs. He puts the roll back again. He looks stupidly at the audience. He grins. He turns to his wife who is reading the newspaper—she rustles it threateningly—and he shrugs again. He wipes his nose thoughtfully on his sleeve.

He grasps the bun then—impulsively. His purpose wavers. He
thrusts the roll hastily in his bathrobe pocket. He crosses his legs.
He whistles tunelessly. He looks increasingly worried and generally
ill at ease. He uncrosses his legs. He pulls the roll from his robe*
and drops it on his plate. He covers his baldness with his hands.
He pats his baldness lovingly like a chimp. He scrubs his baldness,
rubs and scrubs, then drops his arms to his sides in despair.
What are they now but two broken wings! Dead still, stock still,
he sits a moment—statuesque. Then he shrugs. When he shrugs,
it's suddenly—as marble moving. He sighs. He grins stupidly at
the audience. He shrugs. Now he's thinking, pulling at his chin.
He grasps the bun with determination, very bravely—his jaw juts.
He reaches in with his thumb and forefinger formed like tweezers.
He pinches. He pinches. Nothing. He pinches again, a killing pinch
if it's a bug. No, nothing yet. He fishes gingerly . . . fishes . . .
fishes . . . Ah, is it there now? Yes, it is there now, barely betwixt.   .
He tugs. He has it—something. He pulls. He pulls again, and finally
he disengages and slowly draws forth a . . . Well it's not a nose,
of course; it's a sort of unmistakable general idea**. Limp. Ivan—
the husband—squints. Slowly, ever so slowly, slowly in the way the
light of morning clambers up the steepest shade, it dawns on him—

                                                     erases the

what it is. The audience, of course, is having fits.   *swallows the*

darkest
steepest   *Slowly, ever so slowly, slowly in the way light rises a*
wall, it dawns on him—what it is. The audience, of course, is hav-
ing fits. All the bald bastards***, rows and rows of them, are bob-
bing like flowers, like rows of snowy tulips in the wind. At last it

---

* Which should be white and overgrown with roses. It's the shield of this Achilles,
but the gods will not allow my dawdling to describe it. Well, Prince, Genoa and
Lucca are now no more than private estates of the Bonaparte family. No, I
warn you, that if you do not tell me we are at war, if you again allow yourself
to palliate all the infamies and atrocities of this Antichrist (upon my word, I
believe he is), I don't know you in future, you are no longer my friend, my

hits—he's struck—and it is Recognition! *Bun drops.*
The thing flops on the table, white and lanky. He recoils, sliding
his chair, which is on greased casters, half-way across the stage: [bun
snick! After a prolonged silence******, during which both of us sit fall]
as motionless as frightened hares*******, the dialogue commences.

Ivan.   *[timidly]* Dear?

Wife.   *[ignores him, shifts in her chair, shows a little leg]*

Ivan.   *[clears throat, tries unsuccessfully to speak, then does]* Agnes?

Wife.   *[ignores him, shifts in her chair, shows a little more leg]*

Ivan.   *[puts hand over mouth, pops eyes, shoots quick look at audience]*
Hildur?

Wife.   *ignores him, shifts in chair, shows still more leg]*

Ivan.   *[puts hand over mouth, pops eyes, looks imploringly at audience]*
Minnie********?

Wife.   *[ignores him, shifts in her chair, shows even more leg]*

Ivan.   *[gulps, puts both hands over mouth, coasts his chair a few feet*
farther away] Ah . . . *[looks at audience, smiles, shrugs, puts*
finger to lips, then leans over as one does when one is peering
beneath a table or a bureau or a bed, as one does when one is
trying to discover if the car is dragging something, if there is
something under carriage, bush perhaps, a can, a cardboard box
or wind of rusty wire, and from this position, bent like a pin,

** Locke. *Concerning Human Understanding*, Bk. II, Ch. XI, Sec. 9: The use of
words, then, being to stand as outward marks of our internal ideas, mark, and
those ideas being taken from particular things, mark, if every particular idea
that we take in, masticate, and swallow down, should have a distinct name,
names must be endless, names must be endless, names must be endless, names
must be endless; and we must be endless, endless to contain them. Mark—to
prevent this, the mind makes the particular ideas, received from particular objects,
to become general like the spread of a disease, a blight of generals, brassed and
belted, over half the earth, poisoning the ground, destroying the trees; which is
done by considering them, as they are in the mind already such appearances,
separate from all other things, naked, solitary, and apart from every circum-
stance of real existence, such as time, place, or any other concomitant ideas,

peers intently like a soldier at his enemy or a gazer at the stars, peers at his wife with screwed eyes, like Louis Pasteur or some haughty Prussian or a jeweler at gems] Ah . . . *[straightens suddenly and grinning broadly turns and speaks to the audience in a tone at once triumphant and matter of fact]* Olga*********.

Olga. *[bellows instantly]* Wha-a-at**********!

Ivan. *[loses a few more feet]* Ah . . . *[pats his bald spot]* What are you reading, dear?

Olga. *[in a strong but preoccupied voice]* The lost and found.

Ivan. *[with his legs drawn up and clasped in his arms, spins in his chair]*

Olga. *[smashes a hand through the paper, daintily closes the folds of her robe, picks spoon from her saucer and begins, sedately, to stir her coffee***********]*

Ivan. *[cowers]*

Olga. *[face covered by the news, withdraws cup through the shatter, apparently drinks, puts cup back in saucer]*

just as I am, in the spot, amidst my music, when I am parting from my clothing on the stage. This is called *abstraction*, sometimes love, and always the art of writing, whereby ideas taken like a cutpurse from the coat and trousers of particular Beings become general representatives of all of the same kind . . . Thus the same color being observed today in chalk or snow, which the mind yesterday received from milk, it considers that appearance alone, hard, soft, or liquid, elects it a representative of all of that kind, chalkwhite, snowwhite, milkwhite white as the moon on the nail, as the thread that stitches up those endless wounds in the road, and, having given it the name whiteness, it by that sound signifies the same quality wheresoever to be imagined or met with, as in marbles, japonicas, and pearls, as in a joyful day, the innocence of brides, benignity of age, superiority of race, the robes of the redeemed, the bear of the poles, albino seas, their sharks and squalls, their whales; and thus universals, whether ideas or terms, are made, and made immortal, like the sound of a gong or the color of fall in a forest.

A cliche of course *. And did it catch you? Tisk. The image which immediately follows is a fake. Life is full of similar tests *****. Be more observant next time.

Ivan.   [slowly regaining command of himself, he lowers his legs; puzzled now, he stares for a moment at the figure of his wife, then bends a bit in the manner used before*************; finally straightens in defeat, shrugs, coasts in his chair to the apron and speaks to the audience in a strong though confidential whisper] Now which one was it?

Voice from the Audience.   [loudly] Olga*************

Ivan.   [gratified] Ah. [salutes, then propells himself in the direction of the table, perceives what is lying on it, stops with a shudder, spins to face audience, looks blank, shrugs, grins, shrugs, slyly backs his chair toward the table while he speaks***************] Sure,

**** Consequently observe the repetitions of *of course* in such phrases as "It's not a nose of course," and "the audience of course." Strike some one. Guess which. Training . . . training . . . one must keep in training. Write *naturally* instead. That's the trouble, of course. I mean, if people always wrote naturally then we wouldn't have all this cockleaking trouble, would we? but they don't; they won't write naturally, not at all naturally and simply and without contrivance. I mean, the world is a nest of contrivance, nowadays, isn't it?—string and cloth and cottonwood wool and twine, all in a birdy tangle, right? so let's have a little romance, for a change, if that's the mother-buggering trouble with it, what do you say? I say *naturally* is inevitable. So stick *inevitably* in. Now we're all right. Then there's *a cliche of course.* Though close together in the temporal coming onto, these two (now two, for one's been stricken) are nevertheless typologically apart. *Of course* in a footnote and *of course* in the text are naturally not the same *of course.* And you can't claim that if I've merely used a word instead of nobly mentioning it, I've repeated myself. Of course not. No. And this is what is called a literary—a Steinian—stutter, and like any stutter it has the advantage of gaining time, causing your adversary to look away in shame because it shows so often what a word is stuffed with, and how sour it is on the lips, and how badly it goes with the goose. However . . . **Now that I've got you alone down here, you bastard, don't think I'm letting you get away easily, no sir, not you brother; anyway, how do you think you're going to get out, down here where it's dark and oily like an alley, meaningless as Plato's cave? do you think you know the way? well you don't know anything, do you?**

"I SHALL GIVEWAY... I SHALL SAY YES! I SHALL LET MYSELF MARRY HIM—I CANNOT HELP IT!" SHE SUDDENLY WHISPERED, WITH HER HOT FACE TO THE PILLOW THAT NIGHT, ON HEARING ONE OF THE OTHER GIRLS SIGH HIS NAME IN HER SLEEP. "I CANNOT BEAR TO LET ANYBODY HAVE HIM BUT ME!! YET IT IS A WRONG TO HIM, AND MAY KILL HIM WHEN HE KNOWS! O MY HEART— O-O-O-O.

I'm scared of it, I'm terrified. Nasty thing like that. I'm scared to death. *[shivers]* Brrr***************. Suppose you'd found it buried in your breakfast bread; suppose it looked a little like your own, too; how would you feel then? Brrr, eh? *[shivers]* Sure.

not anything, do you? not why you came or how you can back yourself out, and it serves you right, too, mister smart ass, because next time maybe you'll be more careful where you go without a guard or a group of your own kind to yatter a din like indifference around you and safety your ears from me, for I'm a kind of siren and a long wail of warning, you'll see—oh, yes, how I love you now I have you here, why, you're perfect, perfect, you make pennants for gas stations, squirrel tails for cars, yes, sure, you'll beat up nicely, like a malt, oh, yes, how I love you now I have you here —and as long as I talk to you, as long as I threaten you, as long as I bait you, as long as I call you names and blaspheme your gods and tease your pricks and promise to sugar my cunt like a bun for Easter, as long as I grin at you, spit on you, piss on you, continue to hate—as long as I hate like a nigger, with a niggerish hate—then dear brother, lover, fellow reader—then I've got you deep inside me like they say in the songs, fast as a ship in antarctic ice, and I won't need to pinion your arms, lover, butt you or knee, you'll stay, you'll want to, you'll beg me not to go and take my myth, my baffling maze, my sex, my veils, my art away, you simple sucker, down here look-ing for dirt like a schoolboy, down at the foot of this page, between the toes of its body; and I might just carry you on like this, you ass-plugger, carry you on on a flow of words like shit through a sewer, a piece of wasted earth to a hole in the earth, Dante's drain; and there we'll sign on to circle the system again, with the lights in *your* face this time, the eyes *mine* this time, hid by the blaze, and we'll have a real interrogation — you, for a change, in your middle age—and I shall question you closely, kiddo, plane you down to the skin as more than once I've been planed — in a single day, to music, on the Roxy stage, the Paramount, the Palace—and I shall shave you so close and sand you so sensitive, so scarce and smooth, that when I put you at last up in public, in the lights of my lights, then anyone—anyone who's paid his buck in—will be easily able, just by looking, to lick the sweet heart out of your heart, the life from your living, and the daylights out of your cage.

Look—I know I'm old. I'm thirty-five or forty-five or sixty . . . sixty-two or sixty, I should guess******************. Some such. *[shivers]* Brrr. I know I'm past it. Sure. Still, it's upsetting. It's an upsetting thing to think you've lost it. Upsetting. I say it's an upsetting thing, sure, no matter how old you are, why not? To have held on down there for so long like a climber clinging to a cliff, and then to slip . . . *[shivers]* It's sad. Distressing. To have taken all that punishment those years . . . Really distressing. And it's not so easy to tell if it's gone, now, either. ***** But if *bald* goes, *all* g oes—*bob* goes. If *row* goes, *snow* goes. And you haven't a on your bosom. Naked in the guy-light like an emptied se ntence. Whatever that means. ******Prolong this silence until the audience titters nervously. Note: if you found unprinted pages in a book you'd bought, you wouldn't feel embarrassed and need to giggle all the blanks up. You might exclaim: say, look at this, the cheapjakes have left out the dirties. And certainly you'd want your money back. Painters, too, can leave large areas of canvas empty, or spread the same sullen color over great swatches of their precious space, daub after daub identical; but do you suppose, having taken a fancy to it, we could run a little bit of catafalque along: catafalque catafalque catafalque catafalque catafalque catafalque catafalque catafalque? Not on your life. Crepuscular has advocates, as has dirigibility—both nice—but catafalque is best. Along these lines, here's a string of beauties:

catafalque catafalque neighborly mew Ozenfant Valéry leonine nu.

*******Motionless we sat, but did we sit as motionless as frightened hares? Suppose an utter immobility in that. Then we were as still as stones; we were still as a dead man's hat; we were walkless as his bones; we were unweary as the written word, steady as the vestal flame, and permanent as places on a map. Motionless we were, but not as rabbits are, ageless as air; rather as two actors under ban . . . as still as that, as bored as that, as cold. *The hare*

and then terrors appeared in the heavens above. My angel,
I said, my angel, my love. The American War began. For
wasn't I only the stableboy and she the wine-vested lady
of the manor house? And wasn't I in my maleness like a
fencepost driven in her, my arms a circuiting surround,
and she a pale field full of clover, my lips like singing bees?
She slid from her horse and fell against me, cool as the tower
of the horse-trough, elegant in her BVDs, as high above me
on my pole as the flag of our two countries. She slashed me
with her whip and I was scarred with love for life. That's
what I felt start out within me, unrolling from the deep
air in me like a party favor which you blow and as you
blow extends itself to touch another with that secret human-
ness which only paper knows. She whistled tunelessly and
struck me. Ah, Milady, ah my rose, my angel, eagle from
the aerie on the hill, the American manor, the pillared house
on the drafty rise. I shall take you in this horsey darkness,
this stable quiet, this turded territory; I shall topple you to
the straw ground and fill you with myself; I shall bonnet the
head of my masculine thrust with your flowered body, wear
a wig of your private hairs. Put up the horse, you churl,
she said, and curry! Her white teeth gleamed like a pair of
pillows. How small you know how large I am, I thought,
taking one of her long curls in my hand and leading her
away. But have you ever tried to tear a pair of jodhpurs
off? I've only pulled one boot, I cried, shall I screw that?
Oh do, oh do, she hissed, spreading out a blanket for me,
kind at the close, sweet at my finish. With a hoarse shout I
entered the dark sleeve of her slim leg, the long well of her
separated self, oiling all over her purchased skin, but not
like a lotion from the public side, oh no, but like a citizen
who cares for his country does who quietly goes about his
work, turning the great wheels of the wide land, greasing
the skids of commerce. O chambered nautilus, I moaned.
O blindman's buff, she squealed. But I plunged on, the boot
a moon making my tide, while she flicked her whip at some
bluebottle flies and cursed in pure Castilian. I poured my
manhood's pride in her. It was I who spoke, her tongue
was mine. My mother was well born and could have mounted
Emerson instead of the Turk she chose so wantonly to Greek
to. There were no secrets between us then. We threw away
shame like an old stove. We were both burned clean as
dropped ash. We rerose up together. We were three: boot,
stableboy, and she! But times are times, our place was in
our places, so she took her tall proud soul away, alone like a
small cloud on a clear day, although she limped a little up
the gravel path. Still I laughed happily because—from what

Brrr. I'm twenty-two or fifty-two or sixty, and they've crept back into my belly where they came from—the three of them, long ago, I don't remember when—so how should I know, right away, when some Johnny's Tommy pops up in my breakfast bun, whether it was ever mine or what? Disagreeable. I say it's distinctly disagreeable to find a thing of that kind first clock in the morning folded in your sweet roll, sugary, and you just barely up and scarcely open. Sure. You can see the puzzle that I face, my quandary and the turmoil of my mind. Brrr. *[shivers]* I'm not *limped trembling over the frozen grass.* The great frost in *Orlando. And the stars were falling cold, and the smell of hay in the snow, and the far owl warning among the folds, and the frozen hold flocked with the sheep white smoke of the farm house cowl in the river wended vales where the tale was told.* Practice . . . one has to practice . . . keep in practice. *The air bites shrewdly.* Indeed, my feet grew pale in my boots. Love left me, and I was cold as a watercloset in the winter, cold as English sheets would be, cold as plumes of arctic steam, cold, O my heart—O—O—cold, and consequently we jiggled our feet to keep warm; we rubbed our arms and wrinkled our noses; we buffeted our bodies and drank brandy and shouted the cold air out of our lungs: hollah, hollah, hollah—in voices deep as tubas. And I was cold . . . oh not cold as a furnished room is, or an empty bureau, nor as personal, for they are forward compared with me, but cold as a shouting poster, and though my tits shook and my haunches waggled, I was still, too, still as neon, and not with the advertised stillness of death, but with the stillness of someone who has gone away in the midst of an argument, in the center of a sentence, halfway through a caress—hai! hai!—and I could belt them out, baby, not a bugle better—hai! hai!—the words of rude songs and moves of my dances, for I was always gone when I sang them, it was myself I kicked off when I kicked off my spangles—wow, boys, wow—well, frightened hares freeze, they say, but the frighted hare runs.

sure it's even, you know, the one I've been using, that is—mine. I mean maybe it's a friend's, or *[giggles, fingers full across lips like the tips of a fan********************]* one of my wife's friends—how should I know?—or some damn stranger playing the dog in my manger. How should I know? In my spot, who would? Nobody, I'll bet you on it. Nobody would know. Her *[he points behind him]*—she wouldn't. She's walked over my heart a hundred times, like a paving stone, why should she remember every place she's put her foot? *[shivers]* Christ, everyone running around naked and there's never any heat in the joint********************.

[One Minute of Pleasantly Loud and Raucous Music]

******** What's in a name but letters, eh? and everyone owns *them*. Sam says the sound, **sun** or the figures **S, U, N**, are purely arbitrary modes of recalling their objects, and they have the further advantage of being nothing *per se*, for while the sun, itself, is large and orange and boiling, the sight and the sound, **sun**, is but a hiss drawn up through the nose, and a giggle of ink on paper. So use any names you like. Who's in the news? Have a friend in the house? a score to settle? whom do you hate? Or maybe you've thought of a funny one, with dirty undertones. But the language of nature is a subordinate *Logos*, Sam says, that began its life with the thing it represented, and became the thing it represented. Play a joke on that wardrobe mistress, what's her name? Ella Hess. Now the language of Shakespere, Sam says, is neither, but lies gently between, for it not merely recalls the cold notion of the thing, it expresses and becomes part of its reality, so that the sight and sound, **sun**, in Shakespere, is warm and orange and greater than the page it lies on. My apologies. Sam is clumsy even after carpentry, but it is a busy business being the only English critic, and a constant strain on the stomach. I can recall the time Sam

Olga. *[smashes other fist through paper bringing music to abrupt end, grasps her own bun roughly, withdraws it through the shatter *********************]*

Ivan. You appear to have baked somebody's, ah . . . thing-gummy, dear, in your, ah . . . bread.

said, oh he said Fanny or something (Fanny is a pretty good name because later you can say something like, I don't think I'm looking at her Fanny—it always goes over—good theatre is good theatre, so don't get smart), and there was a Fanny present—in the audience, you know. Well this Fanny stands up in her seat and hollars, hey, I don't look a bit like that pig, you jerk, I'm red all day. What a wow! Or maybe she said I'm red all the way, I can't remember. Strange. I should remember. Anyway, we used it often after that, until I saw it was cutting into later laughs. Listen, in this business, all the time, you've got to think.
*********It's funny that a man who can't recognize his own wife behind her 𝕸𝖔𝖗𝖓𝖎𝖓𝖌 𝕿𝖊𝖑𝖊𝖌𝖗𝖆𝖕𝖍 𝖆𝖓𝖉 𝕿𝖎𝖒𝖊𝖘 who isn't certain who she is although she's sitting squatzy at his breakfast table in the same shellfish pink and rosy dawning garden gown she's worn both night and morning close on twenty years, or thirteen years, or two or forty; it's funny that by peering between the bald knobs of her knees like a bandit waiting to bushwhack the Fargo stage—it has applique on its sleeves and bombed off buttons; well, it's funny, though we know he hasn't been inside the cave in a month of Sundays, it's funny—hilarious—that he should recognize her, nevertheless, by the red wig she's using to cover her bunny, because I swear, though I'm not a man, they all look alike, they all look alike, they all look alike to me. *********You must instruct the actress playing Olga to blurt this out at once, almost before Ivan has completed "-ga." I was always very good at it.

Olga. Buns!

Ivan. Buns*********************

Olga. There's only bread in my buns.

Ivan. *My* bun's not entirely bread.

Olga. Bun!

*********** You must instruct the actress playing Olga to emphasize the difference between her fist suddenly smashing through the newspaper, and the modest, dainty way she is to cover her knees, not to mention the delicate refinement of her coffee table manners. I was always very good at it. Incidentally, this is not *Alice in Wonderland*, but real life—the stage—therefore a prop must be prepared which will permit the action called for. A newspaper can be pasted to a piece of folded cardboard just the paper's size. The cardboard must have a hole or passage cut through which the wife's right or left fist (it doesn't matter a damn which, however she happens to be handed) may, at the proper moment, drive. It's best to use the front page of the local sheet wherever you are, but **THE CHRISTIAN SCIENCE MONITOR,** *faute de mieux.*

*********** The gestures of the actors are no more than words, mere words, the commonest kinds (I am hungry; I am tired; I'm full of fear; see me twist the stem of my cocktail glass, that signifies lost love, it signifies my loneliness, it means lust and debauchery; and now I fetch and carry, pour a drink, then drink the drink I pour; I've not arms without my glass of sherry, I lay my head on a tweed and smoky shoulder, then I purr; I inhale, de-ash, stab down, crush out, my cigarette; I sigh into a chair, flop back on the sofa so the pillows muss my hair; ice

Ivan.   Bun.

Olga.   *Your* bread's a bun.

Ivan.   Well, ah, it's not wholly, that is to say, not altogether, straight
        through, bun ***********************

clinks like chain in my glass; figures walk about while I
smile at myself in a mirror; bracelets rattle at my wrists
and jewels hang down swaying from my lobes; in the
modern dream of anxious life, I watch my fingers burning; and there's a thirst in the eye, there's the dry throat
of the ear, the loins yearn, plum plum the nerves, oh
listen to the dreary yatter of the body), and they must be
written, these dreary words, in a nice round hand, so
the audience, all of whom are in the second balcony
straining to see through six penny glasses, can read
them. Ordinary acting is like ordinary prose, placard
after placard

> ## TOILET OF
> ## THE TUILERIES
> # MIDNIGHT

> # NOON
> ## ANOTHER PART
> ## OF THE FIELD

held by helpful Henry in front of belly,
nose, and memory in place of honest clothes.

Olga. Not a whole bun?

Ivan. No mum.

Olga. Better be one.

Ivan. Yes hon.

************ We always used one of the riffle book girls, but don't overdo this voice from the audience bit. Use your head.

************ Rehearse this carefully. Actors can never do more than one thing at a time. Sam's progress should be smooth, a gentle sliding, and he should fetch up to the table as he ends his speech.

************* First he shivers. Then he says brrr. Quite out of joint. Later he says brrr, and following *that*, he shivers. Disconnected. Very amusing. Instruct the actor.

************* Idiots will often say this sentence in a wondering tone, as if they were unsure of themselves or of something. Don't don't don't permit it ****************.

************* It's easy enough to think of them as star*s. It's a little ostentatious, perhaps, like having God's name up in lights, but they run on overlong now, in my opinion, don't you think? Yes, I feel these star*s about to droop. No cantalever lasts forever; which, of course, is why the punctuation has always

When the historian relates events far removed from the age in which he write
When evidence is become scarce, and a ⁄＼ horities are rendered doubtful fro
the obscurities which time has throw ⁄ ＼ them, he ought, above all thing
to be careful that his narration be ⁄ ＼ ly authenticated as the nature
his researches will alow. Strict ⁄ ＼ the eye-witness alone shou
take upon him to transmit far⸗ ⁄ ＼ nd as for the historians, t
coppists, the annotators, wh ⁄ ＼ sessed of no new and ge
uine materials, instead o⸗ ⁄ ＼ nly diminish the autho
ity of their guide; for, ⁄ ＼ bes from the first w
nesses, it may recei⸗ ⁄ **Las Bas** ＼ 'hro' the prejudices
the mistakes of s⸗ ⁄ ＼ nbibe what tinctu

Olga.   All bun.

Ivan.   Then there's another bun in my bun.

Olga.   Another bun?

been put outside—to sort of shore them up. You'll note, I trust, and take to heart, the fact that even in confusion there is a reason for everything. A distinction is usually made between adherence and adhesion. The tendency prevails to confine adhesion to physical attachment, adhérence to mental or moral attachment. Alas, the distinction is not rigorously enforced. As between star*s, you may choose which you wish, though, here, of course, cohesion is the phenomenon meant. We ought not to admire mere size, D'Arcy's book proves. Dinosaurs—terrible lizards, too—remember them****************** ?
***************In addition, the stars interfere with the reading, pester the eye. (Why don't you go to a movie?) More than that, one loses count—which goes with what, what goes with which. All this is true, but don't come crabbing to me about it—do you live in the modern world, or not? Besides, in performance, all difficulties disappear. Anyway, these asterisks are the prettiest things in print. Furthermore, you have no trouble, do you? with charts and tables, graphs or logs. (Go to a movie.) Forward and back, in and out, up and down, we skip about compiling sonorities and sensibles of all sorts and sizes, even to the exter

Ivan.   Yes hon.

Olga.   Bun in your bun***********************?

Ivan.   Yes hon—but not a bread bun.

****************This giggle is what they call a stage giggle; that is to say, a fake giggle, without humor or life.

*****************During this great and moving speech the actress playing Olga must try to keep still, not peep over the top of her paper, stir noisily, waggle her foot or show more of her twot than the situation calls for. This is asking for a lot and will be hard. The chief trouble with the stage is that all the actors normally are alive. Everything else is dead as dumbbells but the actors—and they're alive. It's incongruous. She's also not to wiggle during the music. All you can do is try. Beg. Plead. Still, she'll wiggle. I always did. The stage—it's a mug's game.

*******************All right, cut *two* holes in your cardboard. Nothing easier. How could I know you'd need another? The future is not altogether scrutable. You may die adrift on polar ice, who knows? or marry your mother. How like art is what's left over after life.

********************This is how it should be sung: you appear to have baked somebody's ah . . . thing-gummy, dear, in your, ah . . .

Olga. The bun in your bun's not a bread bun?

Ivan. No mum.

Olga. A bun's a bun, it must be one.

Ivan. You could say it was shaped like a bun. You might. In form, it's bunny.

Olga. *[pause]* Is it round and runny?

breadBUNSbuns. Timing is the essence of the comic. In fact, time is itself comic, nothing funnier. Ha. God. I can barely continue. Ivan begins slowly, understand, tentatively, you follow me? ah, he says, da dee da, bread. Then Olga's loud blat, Buns! comes instantly after, and this is followed immediately by Ivan's meek and quiet, drawn out echo, bunz. Etc.

*********************Contrast is the essence of the comic. Got that? Jesus, it breaks me up. There are all kinds: Olga loud and Ivan soft; Olga tough and brassy, Ivan soft; Olga mountainously rumped and titted, Ivan soft; Olga precipitously cunted, but Ivan soft. The language, too, is sometimes loud and tough and brassy, crude and local, momentary, cheap and jazzy, sometimes euphonious and memorable, swift and flossy, technical and double-jointed. The tone, too, alternates between disgust and dismay, scorn and revulsion, condescension and contempt. Etc.

Ivan.   Well—it's somebody's dummy.

Olga.   You mean it's long and gummy?

*********************Repetition is the essence
of the comic because repetition is mechanical
like love. Wheels and pistons, gears and cams
are comical in themselves. Lying about on
the garage floor, they can be the cause of
giggles. Even the word, piston, is hilarious.
Repeat rocker-arm, for instance—lug. Con-
sider the nomenclature of the tool. Tools are
terribly funny: monkey-wrench and hammer,
pair of pliers. There are shafts, nuts, screws,
and metal nipples. Our girl, the fat girl, me—
I answer a knock on a doorway panel and
who is it? it's the little mimsy-pimsy with the
baggy mantles, dried and old and tired and
still the dream of every male in the theatre
because she's going to widen her walter for
him and he's going to find his leporello big
as the bong of balboa in port au prince, and
the girl asks who are you? who are you, she
says. I'm the pipe-fitter, he answers. Always,
the house howls. Plainly machines have bor-
rowed from the body all these names and
all the body's functions. Now in those circumstances in which the essential humanity
of the human has been called in question, in

Ivan. You've got it! at last you've got it! honey.

Olga. I haven't got it. Give it here.

just those very circumstances, the height of
humor has been scaled. Where the mechanical is seen to shine through the rib-cage (ribs
are repetitious, they shine through the starv-
ing comically) there the funny button has
been pushed; and the reason that, like punch
my judy, I'll punch yours, the reduction of
the human to the mechanical is amusing is
because laughter is social, for example, unlike
self-abuse, and the laugh is a social corrective
like a curtsy or the guillotine, both of which,
though we invented them (we took an age),
have made much shorter work of us. Which
reminds me—I suppose you know the joke
about the very obese Jew whose smoke
was so greasy it stuck in the flue. The
Germans had to slav the stack out
with a bulgar serb of croat they
had hungarian a pole—back and
forth, up and down, round

I salute you,
with great
affection and
regard, for
the last time.

and round, over and over—
until there wasn't a bit of
greece roumanian.✳ ✳ ✳

A cow broke in
tomorrow morning
to my Uncle Toby's
fortifications.

Notions and
scruples were
like split
needles, making
one afraid
of treading or
sitting down,
or even eating.

* Puns. The humor. Wherein? Lies in contrast. You may recall remarks on this behalf. Two independent notions linked by
luck and happenstance. The instrument of union must be vulgar, cheap, and
stupid. Coo of copulation. Pants. It's Effie's phenomenon. The penis, then, in
poetry & prose. Peeing, the penis is in prose. Catafalque. Listen: honeycomb,
quarrier, ringaling, scorch. Sing: susurrus, glycerine, jape. Imposing penis.
Melodious rose. Our pun transforms this overproud presuming Pole into a simple
stick for sweeping chimneys. The sound of his own name has laid him low like a
top hat hitting a ball of snow. The hiss of spit in a furnace. The malice of chimneys.

```
        THE EYE
       BY WHICH I
     SEE GOD IS THE
    SAME AS THE EYE B
  Y WHICH GOD SEES ME.
 MY EYE AND GOD'S EYE A
 RE ONE AND THE SAME
   —ONE IN SEEING,
    ONE IN KNOWING
      AND ONE IN
        LOVING.
```

I believe I was discussing why they call saliva the sweet wine of love, though I can't imagine who "they" are. Would you call saliva the sweet wine of love? Nor should I. Nor should I call it nectar or mead, denominate it cider. It goes back to birds, vomiting in their babies. Perhaps it consists in the ritualization of attack—these bared teeth neutralized. But nothing I say will prevent it, no description mar the quality or lessen the force of its attraction. No one can imagine—simply—merely; one must imagine within words or paint or metal, communicating genes or multiplying numbers. Imagination is its medium realized. You are your body—you do not choose the feet you walk in—and the poet is his language. He sees his world, and words form in his eyes just like the streams and trees there. He feels everything verbally. Objects, passions, actions— I myself believe that the true kiss comprises a secret exchange of words, for the mouth was made by God to give form and sound to syllables; permit us to make, as our souls move, the magical music of names; for to say Cecilia, even in secret, is to make love. How

could the gentlest tremor of our lips cause a weakening of limbs, sur-
render in Samson, if they did not compose a communique of passion?
Consequently, since our thoughts are words in motion, our memories
reserves, our reason regulations for their good and strong employment,

I WOUND NO EARTH WITH PLOUGHSHARES, FAT BEASTS TO FEED THE SHAMBLES; HAVE

the lips that lend expression to the mouth, and the mouth that gives them
tongue, empower our mind, and send it larger to the world. Henceforth,
any intercourse of lips, already a well conceived synecdoche for sex,
should be further and more completely understood to be a sweet con-
clave of heads, and a kind committee in meeting. I'm only a string
of noises, after all—nothing more really—an ar-
rangement, a column of air moving up and down, a
queer growth like a gall on a tree, a mimic of movement in silent readers maybe, a brief beating of
wings and cooing of a peaceful kind, an empty swing
still warm from young bloomers . . . ummm . . . imagine the imagination imagining . . . and surely neither
male nor female—there's nothing female about a
column of air, a gall on a tree—surely both, like
bloomers on the swing's seat . . . so I'm a spiky bush
at least, I like to think, knotty and low-growing,
scratchy though flowering, a hawthorne would suit
me. That I am music when most beautiful (you see?
a man, a mere man, mortal, his death in his pocket
like a letter he's forgotten, could not be that, could

Actually,

it doesn't

matter how t

his scene is pla

yed, for this is wh

at they call a natura

lly humorous situatio

n. It's what you want to

try for: a naturally humor

ous situation. Now a fellow

finding his penis baked in his

breakfast roll like a toad in a bis

cuit—that's a naturally humorous

finding, the very heart of a naturally

humorous situation, and he could say:

say, I think I've found my penis baked

in this roll like a toad in a biscuit, and ever

yone would laugh; they'd laugh, it wouldn't

matter what he said, because it's simply a basi

cally comical condition. If you're in a basically

comical condition, you can do as you please. The lo

vely thing about such a condition, a basically comical

one, is that you can put anything into it you like, only

laughter, simple and true, will ring out. That's in fact, wh

at comedy is made of, if you want to know the whole and to

tal honest of it. A fellow losing his dick somewhere, of cours

se, that could be tragic, anyone can see that could be tragic, but

finding it again, in his billfold possibly, or lying across his co

rnflakes, or coiled in the bottom of his tackle box, that would

be comic, sure as

shooting—comic as

Christmas—a funda

mentally funny fix.

not be beautiful) is nevertheless no help against the licorice I've swallowed . . . imagine the imagination imagining . . . licorice: serpenty, twisted, sticklish, and wallowy. Speaking of the dead, how is it with you? I'm not so good either. Building my own body, you'd think I'd do better, but I've caught a claw in me like the hook of an angler. No. I'm not so good. This tuck that's been taken—it—how shall I say it—well, something has bitten a hole in my lining—some image perhaps, some out-of-work meaning, an unruly and maddened metaphor. It's not ulcerous, you understand—why, I'm a man of music, sweet sounds are piped through my speakers, all very electric like my merry-go-rounder here, into his toes and testicles, a merry glockenspiel of bells, a cheery chorus of ringing—calliopeals . . . then there's the lull that's inside me come evening and all the sweet spoken laymedown beside me like my childhood blanket, no, how could there be, how could there be an ul . . . ul . . . That's very full, that sound. Ulllllll. How do you feel it? How about ul instead of your breast bone? Oh you unfortunate animals—made so differently, so disastrously—dying.

The muddy circle you see just before you and below you represents the ring left on a leaf of the manuscript by my coffee cup. Represents, I say, because, as you must surely realize, this book is many removes from anything I've set pen, hand, or cup to. For example, suppose there were imprinted here, as in letters of love, a pair of lips; could you, by kissing them, let the paper pander between us? Were I to stick my lips as thick with tinted gop as I in fact spread hunks of bread with Scotch cream cheese, I could not reach you—no —or leave a smear on any other portion of your world's anatomy. A wall divides us like the wall which grew between Pyramus and Thisbe on account of the quarrel of their families, except that in my version of the tale I alternately play the lion and the lady's veil. All contact—merest contact—any contact—is impossible, logically impossible (there's not even a crack be- tween us), though I have been invited to kiss many an ass through just such a barrier. But why put a ring in the book? Kiss mine—why not? It can be a map of Dante's seventh circle if you like. Why not? And if you had before you the living hand, the actual stroke, you'd see. Your author writes: *let us sup on the sweets of the world; let us fly through the orchards like birds and sip through the straws of our beaks.* But you observe that his writing marches stiffly up and down like a fence containing cows. Or you receive a billet doux in a careless scrawl you can't read. What sort of billet doux is that, I ask you? It's the hand that speaks; it's the reason that I rhyme; for it's I, over there, on the far side of the icon, pouring another from the pot, at night, in early morning, wintered in, alone; and now I've put my coffee down, the little cream I take curled up in it, and I'm using a sterling silver spoon to smash the curds against the side of the cup, though ineffectually, since they slip away, and in the rush of my spoon through the coffee in pursuit of them (have you seen the sealions at the zoo explode upon their fish?) I create a wave which scarcely crests the lip, still it is enough that shortly, like water which passes so thinly over slate it cannot be perceived, there slides to the saucer and seeps slowly around her whole perimeter some sweet and creamy spill. (I say "cup" because, unless I gravely misjudge, you're not accustomed to hearing harris yet. There's no significance in the name. Sensible attitude. One could wish that others were so wise. harris and langley , they call themselves—a lesbianic cup and saucer. Lesbianic. Lovely. Or take mine. A mere mischance. Who'd have thought that dirty young Joe Slatters would amount to much—amount to a mitten? I don't mind my own—my flattening nomination— either. Actually, I don't mind at all, though of course I wouldn't dare write a line under the shitty thing—under Slatters. Things As They Are by Joe Slatters. The Way We Live Now by Joe Slatters. Impossible—as you can see. (But why not

Oh, I had better plays in mind, as I had better lives.

FERTILE, YET A RAINLESS COUNTRY. THERE'D BE DRIFTING CLOUDS OF MALE BREATH TO COUNT, EACH AN IMAGE OF THE LUNG THAT MADE IT—CLOUDS IN CASTLES, CAMELS, CATHERINE WHEELS —AND OVER EVERYTHING—OVER ME, AS MEADOW—THE SWEET SUN BURNING. I'D FEEL THE SAME SCUFFING, NERVOUS FINGERS I AM

Humphrey Hogg, say; Fleda Vetch, for god's sake? No, I'm not complaining. What's the point? After all, though, the name a man has all his life must do something to him, just as no woman, poor thing, at her birth, receives the name she'll— wedded—go to bed with. What must that do to her? She always knows her own is not her own; that she must borrow, beg of, and be Mrs. Willie Masters, a thing I faced, too, when I went upon the stage as Baby Babs, or when, again, I answered to the name of Olga in a skit—how many names I've had—and it would be easy to lose your soul in the shuffle. Your soul must answer to something. Think if it were nameless. No, no—mine, and yours, and his, must answer; but to what? to what one? If I were to holler up the stairs or down the hall or out a window at myself, what would I say to get my whatjucallit, inner me, the—you know—spiritual person, the deep surviving thing that's bobbing in my body like a bottled pig, to slow, or stop, or turn around, to smile, or wave, or simply and in any way to answer? Slatters *is* a shitty name. Not like Guillaume Apollinaire . And it's led me a shitty life, too. (Notice how I'm slipping through parentheses like fingers into button holes. You don't manage that every day.) "The devil take the puritan!" cried George Staunton, for so we must now call him,—"I beg

Leonora. *[calm surprise with increasing quiet indignation]* Poetry? What's that? What's poetry? I lie here naked, on my back, my legs horsed up at heaven, every gate ajar and all alone,

FEELING NOW, BUT IN ADDITION THERE'D BE THE KISS OF ALL THAT AMOROUS, AMOROUS MONEY. PHILLY, BABY . . . PHILLY. NEVER ANYBODY NAMED SEBASTIAN, SCARCELY A STEPHEN, HARD-LY A LEOPOLD. WELL, WHAT OF IT? WHAT? WHAT OF IT? WALLS. LITTER OF HEAVEN: CLUMPS OF CLOUD, BLOOMING AS CASTLES. OH, HIS LUNGS ARE LIKE HUMPS OF A CAMEL. HIS INSIDE'S BEEN VAPORIZED. HOW THIS MIST OF IMAGES PERFECTLY DESCRIBES HIM. MAYBE THE WALLS. MAYBE THE WINDOWS. GRAY SMUDGE, SMOKE SMUDGE, SPECKS, NICKS, FLAWS: TOWNS AND COUNTRIES COMING INTO VIEW THROUGH THE GRIME. IN THE WALLS, THEN, MY BREATH CLOUDING A MIRROR OR THE GLASS. MY SOUL—A SMUDGE. THEY TEST TO SEE IF YOU LIVE. WILL YOU BLEAR THE

your pardon; but I am naturally impatient, and you drive me mad! What harm can it possibly do you to tell me in what situation your sister stands, and your own expectations of being able to assist her? It is time enough to refuse my advice when I offer any which you may think improper. I speak calmly to you, though 'tis against my nature:—but don't urge me to im-patience—it will only render me incapable of serving Effie." Distracted (have you any notion of my problems?), I sip noisily and stare into space. Ella Bend felt that same warmth, too, many times, when her fingers found her cup, but Ella always

with this shining sample salesman in his polished shoes astride me, and you wish to speak of poetry. All of us aren't better off than I; we're cold, closed in, alone, in some vast public-bordered place where love is called for as you'd call *catafalque* for sausage. We fear our age. We fear our dying and our dying out. Our bellies squeal and rumble and frighten us. Our lungs tremble when we laugh. We burn in our own rage. Husbands and wives have been broken from us. Fathers we despise. Mothers we cannot bear to speak of. And we walk warily among our young as though on nightfall through a

MIRROR? YES . . . YOU DO. YOU BLEAR THE MIRROR, STEP IN THE
DUST, SHOUT—AND BUFFET AIR. YOU BUFFET THE AIR. YOU MOVE.
YOU ARE ALIVE. YOU MOVE—SLIP FROM SMEAR TO BUFFET—LIVE.
AN UDDER DISAPPOINTMENT. SO MAYBE IT WAS THE WALLS, OR
THE WINDOWS, OR THE TREES OUTSIDE THE WINDOWS, THE WALL-
PAPER ON THE WALLS, THE LEAVES, THE LAYERING DUST, THE
FIERCE UNSHADED SUN, THE GRAY KNUCKLES OF STONE, THE
PALE SKY, THE DRIED LEAVES, THE YELLOW CLAY, THE PICKLED
WALLS AND GRAY WINDOWS, THE RUSH SEATS, THE MAGENTA
PHLOX, THE BROWN, THE GRAY AND YELLOW, THE BROWN AND
ORANGE, DOGS, CATS, COWS, AND HORSES STANDING IN CLOUDS,
DEAD AS THE DUST THEY'RE STANDING IN THEMSELVES, OR OUR
PLUMP, WHITE, SINGLE, WOOLLY SHADOWS RUNNING ON THE
GLASSY SKY, LYING ABOUT HAPPINESS LIKE LAMBS AND PUPS AND
KITTENS LIE ABOUT LIFE ALWAYS—CURSE THEIR MAKER—OR MAY-

... swimming in the thin juice of a man's understanding ...

peered longingly in, since the spinning coffee was for her more even than the orbit of an ocean; it was, in addition, the black hat of the heavens . . . oh dear, I am reminded—wondrously reminded—memory is a marvelous, hideous, broom-riding thing —of a hat my uncle had, his only hat, magnetic of snow. Kechel was his name, not that it matters, a fancy undertaker, one who wore full mourning as some of them once did, and this regalia included a tall black topper, a true stovepipe, high and shining,

cemetery. This is not poetry. Only our hate has a high sound. Our work has deserted us. Study and amusement. Faith. Loyalty is lost. That isn't poetry. It's my day off. My husband's got his penis caught between my pilliwinks. There's no space there for poetry.

Carlos.   *[rolling over sleepily]* Hmm?

Angela.   And I should have a man to lean above me, looking as you're looking, pouring his soul from his eyes, and he should say to me

Our life is the time of our body, which is the space of our life.

Philippe.   You have never been looked at before.

Angela.   those things which are forbidden by the motor car,

*BE IT'S THIS LAMP, SO ROSEY-O, OR THIS DAMN SETTEE WITH ITS
BOSSY BUTTONS AND STINKING SLIPPERY LEATHER—IF HE EVER
LOOKED AT ME HE'D SEE I'D BEEN ON MY BACK RIGHT ENOUGH,
HAVING MY PLEASURE, AND LOOKING UP ALONG THE LAMPSTICK
THROUGH THE SATIN OF THE ROSEY-O, THE WIRES CROSSING ABOVE
AN UNLIT BULB, OUT AND UP THE CREAMY CEILING BEYOND THE
GRAY BULB AS IF I WERE LOOKING UP AND OUT ALONG THE
STREAM OF MY OWN EYES, AND IT IS, IT'S MY CURLY FRINGED AND
SATIN ROSEY-O, BOTH MY CLARAS, THAT I'M PEERING UP THE
LAMPSTICK TOWARD THE CREAMY SKY AND LEAD GRAY HEAVEN
FROM, WHILE TAKING, ON MY BACK, MY PLEASURE—PLEASURE,
WILLIE, WILLIE MASTERS, DO YOU HEAR ME? EARS TO THE
GROUND, YOUR LOBELESS YELLOW WOODEN EARS AND TWIN
CANES, LEG STICKS, RUBBER NOSED AND HANDLES WRAPPED—YOU
HEAR ME? I'M GROANING. I'LL GROAN LATER WHEN YOU BEAT ME,
BAT MY BACK ACROSS AND JAB MY RIBS, YES WILLIE, MAKING
LOVE LIKE SOMEONE ON THE STAGE, THE VULGAR BULGAR, MAY-
BE, SO FUNNY IN THE OLD PLAYS, FUNNY AS A CRUTCH; MY GOD,*
which my uncle wrapped in paper and selfishly shut up in a
box he had his oriental servant hide on the shelf of a distant
closet where I would be sure to find it when I sneaked to that

Philippe.   I shall illumine you like God's light illumined the land when

it emerged.

Angela.   the automatic washer,

Philippe.   Though you have played the whore to thousands, and tipped-

up your purse for the police, you shall be so fresh and

newborn

Angela.   and the PTA.

Philippe.   underneath my look, as though you were being

moulded by my gaze. Your nipples turn the color of my eyes.

I see your skin fall clean as new snow everywhere I kiss.

Angela.   His lips will drift so slowly down my back that it shall seem

to him he's spent a weekend on the Concord and the Merri-

mack.

*HOW CAN WE, THOUGH THEY SAY THAT CRIMINALS IN CAMPS, DE-
TENTIONED JEWS AND POLES AND PRISONERS OF WAR, GROW USED
TO PISSING BY THE CLOCK AND SHITTING IN THEIR QUEUES, AND
I REMEMBER HOW MY FATHER AND MY MOTHER ACCLIMATED ONE
ANOTHER, GREW INTO THE OTHER'S COLOR AS NO QUICK CHAM-
ELEON COULD, FOR THEY WERE BOTH THE HIDDEN AND THE
HIDER, SHEATH AND DAGGER, YOU MIGHT SAY, FINDER'S KEEPER,
SLEEP AND SLEEPER . . . AH . . . WELL . . . NONETHELESS, THERE IS
A DIFFERENCE, YES—WHY WILLIE, EVEN YOU NEED BAB'S BARE
BACK TO BREAK YOUR CANES ACROSS, RAGE AFTER IN YOUR
SLIPPERED FEET UNTIL YOU GROW ELECTRIC—NO, IT'S SIMPLY NOT
THE SAME BECAUSE WHEN I AM MASTURBATING I—BY CHRIST—
CALL, WITCH UP, CONJURE IMAGES AND PICTURES, VISIONS, FAN-
CIES, WISHES . . . WISHES! THEY'RE OBEDIENT TO NO ONE. I HAVE
FAERIES STRADDLE ME, AND ANGELS, DEMONS, STALLIONS, DOGS,
AS WELL AS WOMEN. I WILL TRANSLATE, JUST AS BOTTOM WAS,
MY POOR HOMELESS LONELY FINGER INTO ANYTHING. I'LL TACK
IT TO A MAN—MY GOD—TO EVEN ONE OF THEM. PRETEND. AND
COVER MY INADEQUACIES WITH INADEQUACY. HERE, MY LORD, TO
WORK: TO TICKLE FIRST, AND THEN . . . AND THEN . . . TO RUB . . .*

Do not say more
than listening
can explain!

room to visit, tiptoeing the length of the hall, a dinky murk,
to reach it, and there he would let me take the top hat from
its tissues and strut about a bit in front of the mirror like a

I knew a fellow once, entirely imaginary, who rang folks up at random
(he had a scientific mind) to say when they answered, simply: you're
dying, Jack—dying. Or sometimes: you're dying, yes ma'am, dying.
Quick as crack. People can't face it. He was doing them a favor. I, on
the other hand, made so luckily of language—last . . . . even
in a row of dots . . . . in silence . . . . in nothing . . . .
I am. Back now, of course, composing myself again, full of liberty,
creation, and my claw. Now then what's the point? The point is that
you'll never be able to take me seriously: nymph, crawdad, pussywillow,
clientle, Frank. Remember when Frank was a fine name? It's just the
same with me. In language, there's no imagination without music, because music is the movement of imagination. But who can take imagina-

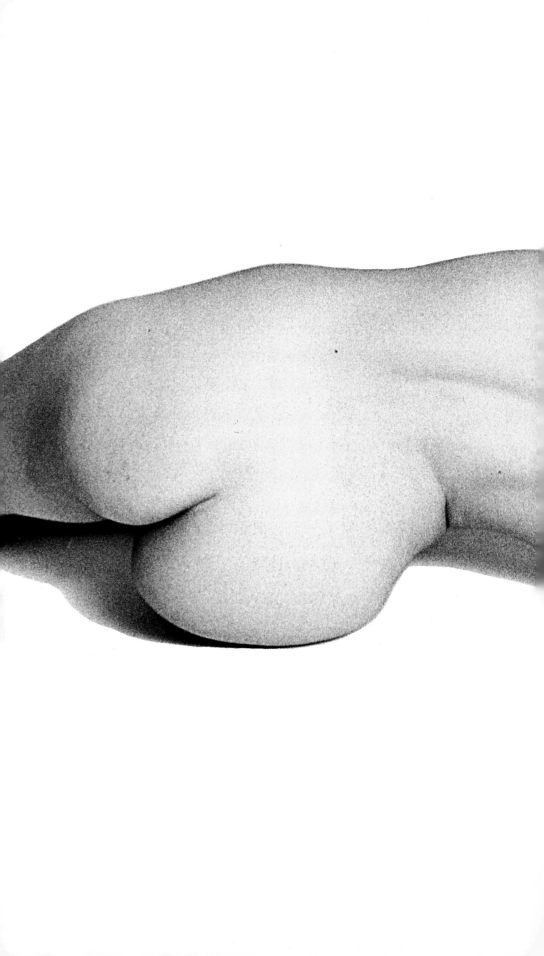

minstrel, doubling myself, until I fell to glooming over the widening well it made, growing so nervous he thought I might wee on his rug, for I did feel I was carrying a quart in a cup, and when I looked steadily into that shining hat, as I always did, much against my will, the darkness would seem to expand indefinitely and draw me down. Then I became afraid to put it on my head again, to cover myself with the soft remorseless color of the blacks, for I thought I should fall straight up if I did. More than once since I've looked into a cloudy sky at night and found myself terrified by the continent of Africa imprinted there. I've fallen to the ground and clutched the earth to hold hard to my dear life. Dear life. What an expression. Sleep, too, is a darkness in which you lose position. This book is closing over me . . . the turning coffee turns, turning Slatters. Ho.

tion seriously when it binds its words with threads of feeling like spiders fill their webs with flies. Not alone because they eat them. You'll never be able to take me seriously, and that's proper, because, well, I'm different, aren't I? . . . because, well, I'm different aren't I? . . . Because, well, I'm different, aren't I? Like a funny foreigner, I wash my undies in the toilet. My wife's name is not Hortense, not possibly. I have *bah* for the hinge of my knee, *lar* for my ear lobe, *lemon* for the lashes of my smoothly sawn eyes. I make none of the regular connections. I tune myself to inner appetites and down-below designs. Facts do not move me. Often I ignore them. Logic is like Lapland. Alone, I never go there. Say—I feel a breeze through my kidneys. It doesn't reach you? Perhaps there's nothing open where you are. So as not to be taken seriously: kelp, whipporwill, sawhorse, hottentot, managerial. Ah. Listen: **managerial**.

The usual view is that you see through me, through what I am really—significant sound—and there at the foot of the steps is a strange man, broad collared and solidly helved, and he's looking up the stairs at his wife with a strange, pained expression on his

Fantast and Pettifog. The river—slow, noiseless, and dark—the Schwarzwasser of Casterbridge—ran beneath a low cliff, the two together forming a defense which had rendered walls and artificial earthworks on this side unnecessary. Here were ruins of a Franciscan priory, and a mill attached to the same, the water of which roared down a back-hatch like the voice of desolation. Brrr. No wonder. I'm in that empty country. God save us all from our fancies and the shapeless night. Thus distracted . . . thus facing a tumultous blank, I am lowering my cup ónto a page. That's the reason I use cream, to soften the blackness, muddy the eyes that stare back at me. So I should like to retain you, my friend, retain you perhaps with a story,

face, and he's saying, putting his hands cautiously to his stomach: I have a funny feeling, right here; and his wife, about to descend, fastening pearls to her throat, says, grunting: you just don't want to go to the Caspars, that's all.

No. I'm not human like you. By the way: have you noticed no one ever takes a proper interest in the penis. I mean the sort you'd expect, considering . . . Poor thing. The very instrument and emblem of the imagination. Gelvin, here, has an irregular tan splotch fastened to the under of it like a grocery sticker.

...these pale emaciated pillars barely standing...

Dear me. Scraps of old poems. They keep wandering around like ghosts, hoping to get used some day. I know of several that have waited years already. Oh not a chance, I tell them. I'll call you. But there you are—they just won't go away. What would you do, if you were a piece of unused poetry?

Well then: there's the speech of science and good sense—daily greetings, reminiscences and news, and all those kind directions how-to; there's the speech of the ultimate mind, abstract, soldierly, efficient, and precise; and then there's mine, for when you use me, when you speak in my tongue—the language of imagination—you speak of fact

but don't you see? Then . . . then . . . then . . . then . . . then . . . then . . . then . . . then . . . then . . . then . . . then you will think of the Ella Bend who walks from me, or of Willie Masters' lonesome wife, they are the same, like me they both hear voices, see when they should not, listen like a pea to its boiling, feel the passions of the pot. There is so much interference, spiritual unease, a good deal of Hardy splashing up, god knows when a wave of him will come from some corner like a wash of absent light, for the whole of literature lies before us, don't you see? like a land we live in, once we've moved there, in the purest figure of our former life, like those glorious Greek

and feeling, order and spontaneity, suddenness and long decision, desire and reservation—all at once. It is the only speech which fills the balloon of the whole man, which proceeds not from this part or from that, in answer to this isolated issue or that well and widely advertised necessity, because, although it may have a focus—some immediate occasion, threat or triumph, fear or hunger, that it is a cry to—nevertheless, it is always —when right, when best, when most beautiful—an expression of a unity, an ideal and even terrible completeness—everywhere rich and deep and full—and therefore—let me warn you, let me insist—can only come from one who is, at least while speaking in that poet's habit, what we— what each of us—should somehow be: a complete particular man. That's why imaginative language can not be duplicated; why it is both a consequence of enormous skill, of endless art, but also a sign in the speaker of his awesome humanity. And both move us. Nothing is omitted: reason, perception, passion, appetite—wound in one expression like wires wind into a cable.

Again there is in every act of imagination a disdain of utility, and a glorious, free show of human strength; for the man of imagination dares to make things for no better reason than they please him—because he *lives*. And everywhere, again, he seeks out unity: in the word he unifies both sound and sense; among many meanings, he discovers similarities, and creates new and singular organizations; between words and things

animals, those heroes, kings, and gods of Plato's amorous country, alive at laws, at love within geometry, who mimic strangely
through a distance, both in form and body, class and category,
each our actual objects; objects physical and filling paired everywhere with evanescent noises quick as bees, birds coming, going,
shadowy as trout, in sudden, brief as fleas; yet only here in this
sweet country of the word are rivers, streams, woods, gardens,
houses, mountains, waterfalls and the crowding fountains of the
trees eternal as it's right they should be; and any mill of sound
I make go round its wheel will roll me farther into it, deepen
its geography and canyon its design; but there's the risk in your
forgetting this—that concepts are their own community—a risk

**he further makes a bond so that symbols seem to contain their objects,
as, indeed, the whale did Jonah, and for Jonah's profit in the end; while
in the other direction (and at the same time), he experiences his speech
as he does himself when he's most fit, when he is *One*—and moving
smoothly as a stream. Imagination is, as Sam said, the unifying power,
and the acts of the imagination are our most free and natural; they
represent us at our best.**

*Got to get description in.
What's this girl look like,
don't we know? And what's
she wearing? Or if she has
shed her clothes, or some
of them, as has been intim-
ated, where'd she put them?
Did she throw, in passion
probably, not caring hoots,
eager for the hot encounter,
her woolly benjamin across a
chair? It's very vague.
This Gelvin fellow, now, for
instance—isn't it? We
could use a pix or two of
him. Cunnilingus or fell-
atio—they have a wide ap-
peal—would do. But please,
be quick, or they'll be . . .*

"I never voyaged so far in
all my life. You shall see
men you never heard of before, whose names you don't
know, going away down through
the meadows with long duck-
ing guns, with water-tight
boots wading through the
fowl-meadow grass, on bleak,
wintry, distant shores, with
guns at half-cock . . ."
We can't make love like that
anymore—make love or manuscript. Yet I have put my
hand upon this body, here, as
no man ever has, and I have
even felt my pencil stir, grow
great with blood. But never
has it swollen up in love.

It moves in anger, always, against its paper.

dress cut from a red and white cotton table
cloth   a tiny check   words fail   but rather
smooth   and soft   distinctly   if only you
could feel it   I had a slim cross-hatching
stripe just like it once when I was younger
in a bathing suit   embracing me like water
those times have drained   my skin has changed
re-arranged its crinkles   o for a smooth soft
water like again   words which sail   white
words   wind skins   fresh northwest dress

that I shall lose you whom I cannot touch, for whom I'm just
a smith of words, out-speaking from my curling cream and
coffee cup some meager message like "hold on, my laces are
undone," or "when's the train for Skokie leave?" but look—see
there—it comes again— the mark! leaf fallen from the cup as
though it had its autumn over, this cup's grief, yes Langley's
love and love ooze, ooze of Harris too, forlorn and brittle pair
of potter's pots. You are a scholar; speak to it, Horatio. My
god, it's not—it is! the image of that lovely twot I ravished last
September in my dressing room at Stratford. Bilitis she called
herself, or some such nonsense, but if spit were sperm she'd
now be brought to bed with twins.   That's how it is.

   **The man of imagination is generally a man of his time, and be-
cause he is, within his medium (again I mention that), capable of life
to a greater stretch than others, he tells us all what it is like to be a
proper man or woman now. Such a thing it is to be a poet . . . and in an
age so shattered out like glass in specialties, so brittle, so irregular, so
plainly seen—as glass is empty of everything but simple passage—that
the role of poet is despised as cheap, unmanly, useless, walk-on, butch.
But he is with us just the same, beneath our breath, beneath our skin,
in all our human possibilities. And when we loose our tongue, then he
will speak.**

You've been had,

haven't you, jocko? you sad sour stew-faced sonofabitch. Really, did you read this far? puzzle your head? turn the pages this and that, around about? Was it racy enough to suit? There wasn't too much plot? I thought the countess something fab. For the nonce. Nothing lasts. But, honestly, you skipped a lot. Is that any way to make love to a lady, a lonely one at that, used formerly to having put the choicest portions of her privates flowered out in pots and vases; and would you complain at having to caress a breast first, then a knee, to sink so suddenly from soft to bony, or to kiss an ear if followed by the belly, even slowly? Only a literalist at loving would expect to plug ahead like the highway people's line machine, straight over hill and dale, unwavering and ready, in a single stripe of kiss and covering, steady on

from start to finish.

This is
the moon of
daylight.

WHEN HE LEAVES HE'LL FORGET SOMETHING. THEY ALWAYS DO. IT'S SUPPOSED TO MEAN THEY WANT TO COME BACK, BUT I CAN'T BELIEVE THAT, FOR I NEVER SEE THEM AGAIN, NEITHER HIDE NOR HAIR; AND THEY ALWAYS LEAVE THE MOST WORTHLESS THINGS, TOO. THIS TIME IT'LL BE HIS RED AND WHITE BOW TIE, AN EMPTY AIRMAIL ENVELOPE, AND A PHOTO OF HIS FATHER. WHAT DID I GIVE HIM THAT HE LEAVES ME THESE? HE EVEN CARRIED HIS SPERM AWAY IN A LITTLE RUBBER SACK. BEMUSED. I GUESS HE JUST DIDN'T KNOW WHAT TO DO WITH IT. DID HE TAKE ME FOR DISEASED? IT ALWAYS LOOKS LIKE THEY'VE MOULTED IN YOU. SNAKES DO. IN NINE YEARS A NEW SKIN. NOT FOR ME. IN A MIN-UTE WILLIE WILL COME STUMPING IN AND WE'LL HAVE TEA IN AUGUST. HE WON'T SHAKE HIS STICKS AT ME JUST YET. THEY'RE SO FORLORN WHEN THEY FINISH, AS THOUGH THEY'D LOST A LITTLE OF THEIR LIFE WHILE COUNTING IT—THEIR DIME ON THE WAY TO THE STORE. THE DUMPLINGS ON MY CHEST CALL THEM TO DINNER OR TO SOME APPOINTMENT, AND THEIR EYES FLY NOISILY AGAINST THE WINDOWS. THEY FUMBLE UP THEIR BUTTONS, ZIP THEIR ZIPS, AND IF THEY'D PAID ME SOMETHING, SAY A FIVE SPOT, THEY COULD SMILE UPON MY SMILES OR SAY GOODBY PERHAPS; BUT NO, IT'S FREE, THEY'RE DONE, THE HOLY OFFICE OVER, AND THEY TURN THEIR BACK ON ME, I'M WHAT THEY'VE LEFT, THEIR TURDS IN THE TOILET. ANYWAY, I MUSTN'T WONDER WHY THEY DON'T RETURN. MAYBE I SHOULD PUT A TURNSTILE IN. I TOOK MY CLOTHES OFF ON THE STAGE—NAKED PLAYED THE FOOL, THE NAG, THE SHREW— FOR MONEY. MY DEARS, I WAS BORN A PRO, A PRO, SO REALLY NOTHING'S CHANGED.

What should I call you: huntress? chaste and fair? My sterile star? the emblem of my afternoons. As you see, its center's empty, no glow there. And I am lonely. This stupid creature who just now has left me, whom I favored with my charms, a bosom born but thirty years ago and plump as ever, round as a pair of pies when I lie down, has not come and gone upon me harmlessly, although he put his penis in a plastic bag like something you'd buy frozen at a grocery; for he did not, in his address, at any time, construct me. He made nothing, I swear—nothing. Empty I began, and empty I remained. O dears, I know—it was a hollow victory, hollowing him. Still, I'm always good, mum, always fine; I went no farther with him than the suburbs of my body. Thus we never touched, nor would have, though he feared me greatly, when we fucked. Afterward, he carried his seed off safely in a sack. Well, what the hell—he's some hybrid maybe, strain of Burpee, supergiant, extra early, so I should, had he not worn his celloguard, have been but seven months to bud, a week to bloom, and three more days to fruiting.

This moon, then, is something like me. For one thing, I'm an image. I still reflect the spots which lit me all those years. I turned in them, revolved—you know the way it was—I shook. My hands felt for me, slowly slid along my thighs so every customer could dream his own were sliding slowly in that sliding place. Poor gentlemen. I'd like to laugh at them because I cannot cry. Well, I'm no longer the nooky-look-see sort of tease I was, I can tell you that. I used to sweep my nipples clean and blacken the stage in a single gesture. Their own straining undid them, you know—the starting of their eyes, the stare; it was never as dark as it seemed. Anyhow, that's the way it worked: I gave them tantalizing glimpses, passed behind clouds constantly, or simply changed my shape—into a mouth, to a curl, to a shiver.

Sometimes an actress, shut up in her dressing room, loses herself in her role and emerges a queen; but I moult my dress and panties on the stage and only wish it were another, not myself, that I discover. Then I dispose my flesh to pretense like a paper napkin; put on passion as I put on paint and powder; try to believe I've flung my body in the wings and out of seeshot with my spangles. Still, wherever I am, I'm lonely. Night frightens me. I do not watch the moon there. Only by daylight, when it seems almost a tissue, frail and antic, can I bear it and its scrutiny. I want to have familiar things around me when a man is on me; he'll be too strange, too foreign for me, otherwise. Something unforeseen might happen. It must have the carpet, its diamonds interlaced and wound with silver leaves and flowers bursting into bloom like bombs; I must have the scratches with which my plum and tawny colored pumps have enlivened the coffee table; I must have that green glass vase the daffodils die in, the books by Miss Pearl Buck I glued up in a stack to stop the door, the photographs of castles which threaten to topple on the radiator, the brass fly, the lacquer dish, the cloudy face of a clock lamp; it is a weakness, but I must have this stupid black slick leather-covered couch, the tarnished fire-irons and the sloping piles of tattered magazines I used to cut designs and paper ladies from, the dull bleak busy walls like this man's arms around me; I must have the painted ice cream chair, the drop-leaf table, the idle doilies, the dirty ashtray, the pewter mug, the pretty pillow and its corner tassels, and the downcast china baby doll which says *enfant de France*. These things crowd into my eyes while *it* is going on—the jouncing and the ramming; they press close, they fill me better than a man can, they speak to me of value, weigh me down, my fancy cannot sail itself to Spain, or dub me a Balkan princess, while these buttons dent my bottom or the whiskey snickers in my glass. So I make my love in daylight, in the sight of all their smicker, even though the moon is shining. The watch won't change the gallop of my cowboy, or the scintillation of his hair; but my mind can't bolt into the flat dead-open middle of the night so easily or often over these few fences. It's still and quiet there. Sometimes I hear late buses groan, or a lone cab corner noisily, but mostly, though I hug my covers close, my own insides, like craven cuttlefish, cloud ink around me. Oh, be assured that on ocassion I am brave; I read John Dryden, hear his shepherd say,

> The rest I have forgot; for cares and time
> Change all things, and untune my soul to rhyme.
> I could have once sung down a summer's sun;
> But now the chime of poetry is done;
> My voice grows hoarse; I feel the notes decay,
> As is the wolves had seen me first today . . .

and make a start against the darkness anyway. Then I draw my dreams—as if a few white lines brought daylight to a blackboard—successively from star to star in vast dim figures like the zodiac's. To write on such a wall, my honeys—yes, my sweets, my dears—inhibits smirch, enlarges all your members but your soul's conceit, which it ties small with fears like Chinese feet.

When a letter comes, if you will follow me, there is no author fastened to it like the stamp; the words which speak, they are the body of the speaker. It's just the same with me. These words are all I am. Believe me. Pity me. Not even the Dane is any more than that. Oh, I'm the girl upon this couch, all right, you needn't fear; the one who's waltzed you through these pages, clothed and bare, who's hated you for her humiliations, sought your love, just as the striptease dancer does, soliciting male eyes for cash and feeling the light against her like a swelling organ. Could you love me? Love me then . . . then love me . . . Yes. I know. I can't command it. Yet I should love, if ever you would let me, like a laser, burning through all foolish ceremonials of modesty and custom, cutting pieties of price and parentage, inheritance and privilege, away like stale sweet cake to sick a dog. My dears, my dears . . . how I would brood upon you: you, the world; and I, the language. You should feel me moving, my mouth moving, like your better feelings rising; sheer elation—joy—would lighten you like gas in a balloon; but how many men would screw if there were any likelihood their spermatozoa might, like famished millions in rebellion, turn back to storm the heaven of their manufacture? Why not? So much of it's self-love. Why not infect yourself with your infections? No sacks to send your seed to safety in. Frankly, Mr. Gelvin—you *are* Mr. Gelvin, aren't you? Gelvin of the shining helm and sample shoes?—well, frankly, Mr. Gelvin, far better you than us.

I am that lady language chose to make her playhouse of, and if you do not like me, if you find me dewlapped, scabby, wrinkled, old (and I've admittedly as many pages as my age), well sir, I'm not, like you, a loud rude noise and fart upon the town. But let's not quarrel. Though you'll not be back, your brother will. Tell him he is responsible for me, and that I give as good as I receive. If he will be attentive, thoughtful, warm and kind, I shall be passionate and beautiful. He should prepare to leave particularities behind, abandon envelopes and photos, trophies of all kinds, the ringing silver voice in which the tinny actor hides, his contraceptive sacks, his dirty pipes, his damn bow-ties; for I shall be quite singular enough to suit sly John the Scot himself, that canny philosopher who taught that Truth, though One, was irridescent as a plash of oil, and varied endlessly from spot to spot; John Scot, the wise, you may remember, who was murdered by his students, so the story goes, at the Abbey Malmesbury, with their pens; why, I can't imagine, for it was he who, dying of his pen wounds, said: how close, in the end, is a cunt to a concept—we enter both with joy.

Then let us have a language worthy of our world, a democratic style where rich and well-born nouns can roister with some sluttish verb yet find themselves content and uncomplained of. We want a diction which contains the quaint, the rare, the technical, the obsolete, the old, the lent, the nonce, the local slang and argot of the street, in neighborly confinement. Our tone should suit our time: uncommon quiet dashed with common thunder. It should be as young and quick and sweet and dangerous as we are. Experimental and expansive—venturesome enough to make the chemist envy and the physicist catch up—it will give new glasses to new eyes, and put those plots and patterns down we find our modern lot in. Metaphor must be its god now gods are metaphors. It should not be too cowardly of song, but show its substance, sing its tunes so honestly and loud that even eyes can hear them, and contrive to be a tongue that is its own intoxicant. Full of the future, cruel to the past, this time we live in is so much in blood with possibility and dangerous chance, so mixed with every color, life and death, the good and bad homogenized like milk in everything we think—new men, new terrors, and new plans—that Alexander now regrets his love of drink; Elizabeth, that only Queen, paws for her wig to seek employment; and the swift Achilles runs against his death to be here. It's not the languid pissing prose we've got, we need; but poetry, the human muse, full up, erect and on the charge, impetuous and hot and loud and wild like Messalina going to the stews, or those damn rockets streaming headstrong into stars.

HERE
BE
DRAGONS

YOU HAVE
FALLEN
INTO ART
—RETURN TO
LIFE

"... using a sterilized side of ... coffee down the li..." in early morning

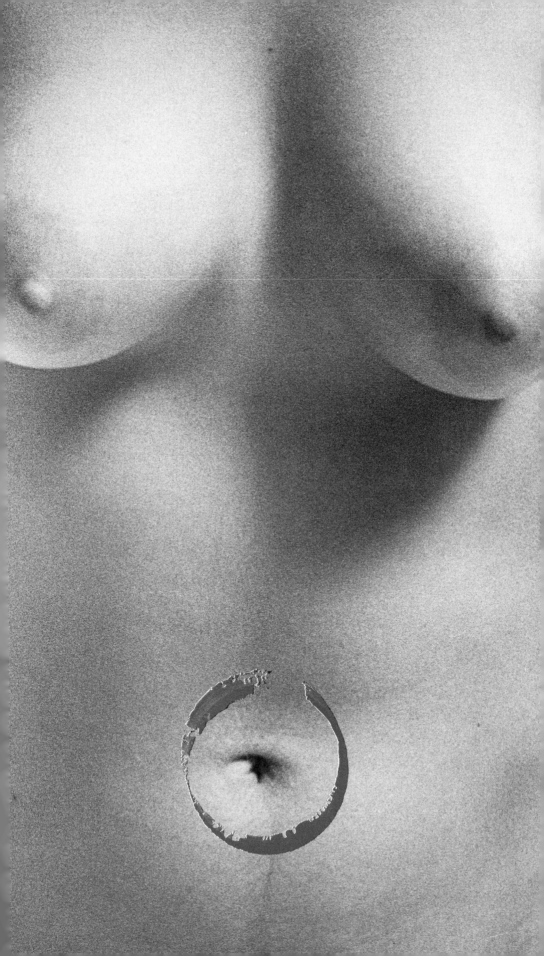